Emily H and the Enormous Tarantula

"There he is! The Villainous Fiend!"

The Professor was striding towards his laboratory. Emily H saw that he had his killing bottle, and realized at a glance she was too late to save the tiny spider in it.

"Murderer!" she shouted.

The Professor shook his fist. "For the millionth time, you odious child, I am not a murderer! I AM A WORLD FAMOUS SCIENTIST!"

Watch out for:

Emily H and the Castle Thief
Emily H Turns Detective
Kara May

Dare you try a Young Hippo Spooky?

Scarem's House
Malcolm Yorke

The Screaming Demon Ghostie
Jean Chapman

Four Young Hippo Magic stories to enjoy:

My Friend's a Gris-Quok
Malorie Blackman

The Little Pet Dragon
Philippa Gregory

Broomstick Services
Ann Jungman

The Marmalade Pony
Linda Newbery

Ready for a Young Hippo Adventure?

Henry to the Rescue and Other Stories
Ruth Silvestre

Young Hippo Adventures for confident readers:

The Outfit Series –
The Secret of Weeping Wood
We Didn't Mean To, Honest!
Kidnap at Denton Farm
Robert Swindells

K ARA M AY

Emily H and the Enormous Tarantula

Illustrated by John Bendall-Brunello

Hippo

Scholastic Children's Books,
Scholastic Publications Ltd,
7–9 Pratt Street, London NW1 0AE, UK

Scholastic Inc.,
555 Broadway, New York, NY 10012-3999, USA

Scholastic Canada Ltd,
123 Newkirk Road, Richmond Hill,
Ontario, Canada L4C 3G5

Ashton Scholastic Pty Ltd,
P O Box 579, Gosford, New South Wales,
Australia

Ashton Scholastic Ltd,
Private Bag 92801, Penrose, Auckland,
New Zealand

First published by Scholastic Publications Ltd, 1995

Text copyright © Kara May, 1995

Illustrations copyright © John Bendall-Brunello, 1995

ISBN 0 590 55831 5

Typeset by Contour Typesetters, Southall, London
Printed by Cox & Wyman Ltd, Reading, Berks

10 9 8 7 6 5 4 3

For my mother

Chapter 1

Emily H

Emily Annabel Florentine Hatchett had long fair hair with a bow at the back, and she looked like an ordinary child.

But Emily wasn't an ordinary child.

To begin with, her favourite food was cold steamed spinach.

Ms Lavender Pottle told her no other child would eat it.

"I know it looks like green slime," said Emily. "But it can't help that, and I totally adore it."

Emily didn't go to school (she had lessons with Ms Pottle) and she didn't see her parents every day or even once a week. They were mostly away on "important business" and she was left at home.

For Emily, "home" wasn't a house or a flat or even a caravan. She lived in a castle. It was a small castle with a fountain which had a lion in the middle, and Emily loved it.

"It's my favourite place on the planet," she said.

One day she was sliding down the castle banisters, which was one of her favourite things, while Ms Pottle sat by, trying to knit herself a scarf. (It was more holes than scarf.)

Suddenly Emily jumped down beside her.

"I've decided to do something with my name," she said.

"Do what?" twittered Ms Pottle.

"I'm going to take the 'H' from

'Hatchett' and put it with Emily."

Emily dipped her fingers in a vase of daffodils. Ms Pottle was never sure what Emily was going to do next, and wondered if she was going to eat them. But she sprinkled the water over her head and declared:

"From now and forever I am Emily H."

A few days later cards were delivered which read:

MY NAME IS EMILY H.

There were also new name cards for Ms Pottle. She looked at them in dismay. There was just one word printed on them:

POTTLE.

"My name is Ms Lavender Pottle," she squawked.

"But Pottle is most unusual," said Emily H. "You could be the only Pottle in the world. True or false?"

"True, I suppose," whimpered Pottle. She was a wispy little woman who wore her hair in a bun from which the hairpins were forever falling out. "But I shall miss my Ms and Lavender," she whimpered on. "It makes me feel quite faint."

Emily H quickly handed her the smelling salts.

"Take a sniff, Pottle, you'll soon feel better. But now I must leave you. I'm expected in the attic."

The attic was Emily H's favourite room in the castle because her favourite creatures lived there. She raced up the stairs, two at a time, and flung open the attic door.

"Here I am, my darlings!"

From the rafters, through cracks in the walls and up through the floorboards a variety of spiders came running towards her. They crawled up her legs and over her arms. Some even perched on her head.

"You're always so pleased to see me!" beamed Emily H. "But now sit still, and I'll tell you a story."

It was a story she'd made up herself
about a country where the people were so
stupid they couldn't tie their shoelaces,
and were ruled by a government of genius
spiders.

She was just saying "The End" when
Pottle came to fetch her for tea.

"Cold steamed spinach?" asked Emily H.

Pottle sighed. "Yes, dear. Cold steamed
spinach."

Every night Pottle prayed, "Dear God,
Please make Emily H into an ordinary

child with an ordinary name who'd sooner lose a week's pocket money than eat cold steamed spinach or have spiders crawling on her.

"But perhaps," mused Pottle, "she's not an ordinary child because she doesn't know how."

Pottle didn't often make a decision by herself, but she decided to ask some local children to tea to set Emily H an example of ordinary-child behaviour.

She made a list of the things they liked to eat: crisps, hamburgers, blood red ketchup, gooey chocolate cakes, raspberry ripple ice-cream.

She also made a list of the things they liked to play on: swings, climbing frame, see-saw.

The day of the tea arrived. The children tucked in, but Emily H didn't get the idea at all. She fed her crisps to the dog, and put ketchup on the swings. Then she led the children up to the attic.

"As a special treat," she said, "I'll let you play with my darlings."

She led the way up to the attic. As soon as she opened the door, the spiders came running. The children screeched and screamed and fled. Pottle begged them to come back, but they wouldn't.

"Oh dear!" she twittered.

Emily H looked at her with concern. Pottle was shaking so much that all her hairpins fell out.

"Those children have frazzled your nerves," she said. "But don't worry, I won't let them in my castle again."

She sent Pottle to bed with her smelling salts and hot-water bottle.

"Now I must be off!" declared Emily H.

Pottle trembled under her duvet. "Off where?"

Emily H's face was cold and grim.

"I'm going to spy on my Number One Enemy, Professor Percy Pinkerton!"

Professor Pinkerton was a world famous expert on spiders. It was the way he studied them that made him Emily H's enemy. First, he killed them in his killing

bottle. Then he cut them up to examine their insides, and went on to write a book on what he'd found.

"Spying on him is my least favourite thing, but it must be done," said Emily H. "An innocent life could depend on it!"

She left Pottle sniffing at her smelling salts, and raced off to her tree house on the far side of the castle grounds. The Professor lived next door, and the tree house overlooked his garden. She peered down through the branches.

"There he is! The Villainous Fiend!"

The Professor was striding towards his laboratory. Emily H saw that he had his killing bottle, and realized at a glance she was too late to save the tiny spider in it.

"Murderer!" she shouted.

The Professor shook his fist. "For the millionth time, you odious child, I am not a murderer! I AM A WORLD FAMOUS SCIENTIST!"

"Someone should put you in a bottle, and see how you like it!"

The Professor opened his mouth to roar back a reply, but Emily H didn't wait to hear it. She ran back to the castle and fetched some paper and crayons. Pottle was delighted.

"What are you drawing, dear?" she asked.

Emily H was exceptionally good at drawing, but complained it was more boring than exciting and mostly, she wouldn't bother with it.

Perhaps the tea has turned her into an

ordinary child, after all, thought Pottle. Eagerly she peered at the drawing. She had hoped for a flower or a sunset. But it was Professor Pinkerton in a bottle with the lid screwed on, tightly.

"It's what he deserves," said Emily H.

The next morning she was showing the drawing to the attic spiders, when she felt a sudden shiver shoot from head to toe. How strange, she thought. It was a hot day, so it couldn't have been from cold. She was still puzzling over it when there

was a ring at the castle bell.

On the doorstep stood a squat, sturdy man with so many tattoos on his arms that none of his skin showed through.

"It is I, Edwards, myself!" he declared.

"Enter and welcome," said Emily H.

Edwards was her Secret Agent. He also kept house for Professor Pinkerton. He loathed the Professor almost as much as Emily H, but it was the only job he could find because of his tattoos, and he needed the money. (He was saving up to take his Old Mum on a round-the-world cruise.) It gave him great satisfaction, however, to report to Emily H on what her enemy was up to.

"There's been a happening as I surmise that you, Herself, will be wanting to know

about, concerning Old Fur Face and a tarantula," he said.

"Quickly, tell all!" urged Emily H.

Edwards had a roundabout way of telling things. But Emily H was used to it. She quickly grasped what had occurred:

Earlier that morning, the Professor was reading the paper when a headline caught his eye:

RECORD-SIZED TARANTULA SPOTTED ON TABLECLOTH!

A couple on their honeymoon in South America were having a picnic in the jungle when a tarantula of enormous size walked on to their tablecloth. Where it went next, they couldn't say. Terrified, they'd fled back to their hotel.

The Professor hurled the paper in the air. He was sweating with excitement. Tarantulas were the biggest spiders in the world! This one could be the biggest of the biggest! He could write a book about it and be more famous than ever.

"Edwards, you witless turnip, pack my bags," he bellowed. "I'm going to South America."

"I won't tell you my thoughts on being called a witless turnip," Edwards said to Emily H. "Suffice to say, that I drives Old Fur Face to the station, then I comes here, to see you, Herself, Emily H. Report finished and concluded."

"Thank you, Edwards."

Emily H's face was grave. Now she knew what had made her shiver. She had sensed

the tarantula was in dire peril!

"I must save it from the Villainous Fiend. Come, Pottle," she said. "We must leave at once for the jungle."

"The jungle! Oh dear!"

Pottle began to faint, but Emily H stuck her smelling salts under her nose, and asked Edwards if he'd drive them to the station.

Edwards beamed. "In Old Fur Face's car, on his petrol? My pleasure!" he said.

Soon after, Emily H and Pottle were on a plane, heading for South America.

Chapter 2

The Theraphosa Leblondi

Emily H and Pottle had been in the jungle for a week, looking for the record-sized tarantula.

"Wait for me!" squawked Pottle. "The monkeys have stolen my hat."

Emily H sighed. Pottle hadn't stopped squawking since they'd arrived. "The monkeys are only playing. They always give things back. There! What did I tell you!" she said, as the hat landed plonk! on Pottle's head.

"It nearly knocked me out! Oh dear," whimpered Pottle. "I've tried to like the jungle, but it doesn't agree with me."

It wasn't just the monkeys. The food upset her tummy even more than cold steamed spinach. Then there was the jaguar that she'd met face to face when

she was gathering wood for the camp-fire. Her scream had scared off the jaguar but it had scared her too, and she'd fainted.

"Please, dear, can we go home?" pleaded Pottle.

"And what about the tarantula?" demanded Emily H. "If we leave it here for the Professor to find, he'll kill it and cut up its poor darling corpse. True or false?"

"True," said Pottle.

"You wouldn't want its blood on your hands?"

Pottle shook her head.

"Then let's have no more talk of going home," said Emily H. But Pottle started squawking again. Now it was her feet. "Please, dear, can't they have a rest? If they don't, my blisters will burst."

"All right, just five minutes," said Emily H.

Pottle sat on a log and took off her shoes to cool her feet in the river. But the log was a crocodile. It suddenly plunged into the water with one of her shoes and began to eat it.

Pottle's screams echoed round the jungle.

"For goodness' sake, Pottle! Your shoe
hasn't got your foot in it. The croc's not
eating you. True or false?" asked Emily H.

"True," squeaked Pottle.

"Then there's no need to fuss. We're
on a life-and-death mission, remember?
Put on your spare shoes. And hurry!"

The only spare shoes Pottle had were
her wellies. She put them on and followed
Emily H into the darker depths of the
jungle.

As the days passed, however, Emily H found it a struggle to keep up the search. Her knees ached from crawling. Her hands were all scratches and she counted fifty-one bites from bloodthirsty mosquitoes. To keep her mind off her aches and itches she decided to say the alphabet backwards.

"M, L, K," she was saying, when she came to a bushy tree-fern.

She stopped to see if the tarantula was in it and found herself facing a beard. The beard dropped as the mouth that owned it gaped wide in surprise.

"It's the odious child!" snarled the Professor. "What are you doing here?"

"The same as you, Villainous Fiend!" retorted Emily H.

The Professor smiled a gloating smile. "You haven't a hope of finding the tarantula and I'll tell you for why!" He'd been round the villages and offered a huge reward for whoever found the tarantula.

"And don't think of doing the same, odious child. Whatever reward you offer, I'll double it!" he said.

Emily H held her nose. "Come on, Pottle, there's a smell around here I don't like!"

Pottle's hopes lifted. "Are we going home?"

"No, Pottle, we are not. We are going to the police," said Emily H.

They found a police station in a nearby village. Señor Pedro was in charge of it. Emily H introduced herself.

"I'm sure you'll be pleased to meet me, Señor. My name is Emily H. Here is my card to prove it. I'm not an ordinary child," she said. "True or false, Pottle?"

"True," said Pottle.

Suddenly, Señor Pedro's eyes snapped open. He'd seemed to be asleep under his sombrero. It was a trick he used so he

could check people over without them
knowing – he was fussy about who came to
his village.

"Do you like cats?" he demanded.

"But of course!" replied Emily H.
"They're my favourite creatures, after
spiders!"

"I adore cats too!" chimed in Pottle.
"Well, little ones!" she added, remembering the jaguar.

Señor Pedro smiled. "Cats are my heart's delight. You are welcome to my village. What can I do for you, Emily H?"

"It's more a case of what *I* can do for *you*. I come with important news!" declared Emily H. "In your jungle is a Villainous Fiend. A murderer, in fact! He's fled from our country, Señor. Do you want him running loose in yours?"

Now Señor Pedro was wide awake. He whistled through his teeth, and the villagers came running.

"We have a murderer in our jungle! Find him!" he commanded.

Emily H did a quick sketch of the

Professor so the search party would know what he looked like. Señor Pedro was so taken with it, he asked her to do a sketch of him. Emily H had just finished it when they heard a noise that sounded neither animal nor human. A few minutes later, the search party returned with the protesting Professor, tied like a goat to the end of a rope.

When he saw Emily H, he all but choked on his beard in rage.

"This is all your doing, odious child!"

He turned in a fury on Señor Pedro.

"I'm not a murderer, you nincompoop! I am a World Famous Professor!"

Señor Pedro raised an eyebrow. "Prove it," he said.

"I will!" steamed the Professor.

"In the meantime, I'll keep you in here."

Señor Pedro unlocked the one and only cell and pushed the Professor in. The cell was small and already occupied by two garlic-chewing brigands and a pickpocket called Marco who'd picked up some fleas in the local market which were hopping all over him.

"Let me out!" screeched the Professor. "You can't lock me up with these riff-raff!"

Señor Pedro took a puff on his cigar

with a smile that said, "I can and I have."

"That's got rid of him for a while," said Emily H. "Well done, Señor. Now we must get back to the jungle."

"Can't I stay here?" pleaded Pottle. The riff-raff looked terrifying and so did the Professor with angrily gnashing teeth, but unlike the croc or the jaguar, they wouldn't eat her.

"I'd feel safer in prison," she said.

Emily H regarded her sternly. "I don't think my parents would be happy if they got to hear about you putting yourself in prison. True or false?"

There was just one answer to that! Pottle picked up her knapsack.

The next day the rainy season began. Pottle was glad she was wearing her

wellies. "You should wear yours too, dear. You'll catch a chill."

Emily H grinned. "I don't want a chill, so why should I catch one? And no chill would dare catch me!"

But a chill caught Pottle and she had to spend the day in her hammock with her hot-water bottle. Emily H was fetching some more water from the river to heat up for it on the (very smoky) fire, when she heard Pottle's loudest scream so far.

"What is it now?" she sighed.

She found Pottle lying in her hammock, white and still.

"Oh no! She's passed out again," said Emily H.

She was about to throw the water over her to bring her round, when she saw

something sitting on Pottle's chest. Emily H realized at once what it was. An enormous tarantula! Not any enormous tarantula, but a theraphosa leblondi, the largest breed of spider in the world.

Emily H gazed at the tarantula. She knew the largest one on record measured twenty-five centimetres. "Do you mind if I measure you, my sweet?" she gently asked.

The tarantula spread out its legs, making itself as large as possible, and looked up at her with bright twinkling eyes.

Emily H took out her tape measure.

"Oh!" she said.

For one whole minute, Emily H just sat. Then she picked up the smelling salts and held them under Pottle's nose.

"Take a whiff, Pottle. This is no time to faint. It's a time for total rejoicing. I've found the tarantula!" said Emily H.

Chapter 3

Mission Accomplished

The rain had stopped and the fire had stopped smoking. Emily moved in closer. But not too close! The tarantula was sitting on her lap.

"Thirty-five centimetres! That's what he measures, Pottle! True or false?"

"It was true the last time you asked me. I don't think he's grown or shrunk since," twittered Pottle. The shock of finding the biggest spider in the world sitting on her chest had got rid of her chill, and now she was feeling quite perky.

Emily H stroked the tarantula's hairy back. "You're the biggest spider on record. But you're in mortal danger, my sweet." She told him about Professor Pinkerton. "If you stay here, as sure as the parrots squawk, the Villainous Fiend will find you.

If you come home with *me*, I'll guard you
with my life. But only if that's what you'd
like."

"But he belongs here, dear," said Pottle.
"I think the government will want him to
stay in their jungle."

The tarantula leapt up and ran round in
a circle. Then he climbed into Emily H's
knapsack.

"There!" said Emily H. "He wants to
stay with me. True or false?"

"True, I suppose," sighed Pottle.

"The government can like it or lump it!
You'll want for nothing," Emily H said to
the tarantula. "To begin with, I'll give you
a name."

"But it's got one, dear. Thera . . . I forget
what," said Pottle.

Emily H turned to the tarantula. "Pottle's mind sometimes is more absent than present. But I've thought of a name that's got theraphosa's 'TH' and the 'E' and 'O' from leblondi. Is that a name you'd like?"

The tarantula's eyes twinkled and he waved his right legs. Emily H knew this meant, "Yes."

"I hereby name you Theo," she said.

Pottle gave an excited squawk. "I could remember that, dear. I was once engaged to a man called Theo. But I lost him at the races and never found him again."

Emily H and Theo looked at each other, and then at Pottle.

"I think it's time we left the jungle, and went back to the castle," said Emily H.

A walk and a bus and a train took them to the airport. When they boarded the plane, Emily H sat with Theo asleep in her knapsack on her lap. The plane was about

to take off when a nasty surprise sat down
near her: Professor Percy Pinkerton!

"Oh, no!" she gasped.

The Professor had proved who he was,
and Señor Pedro had had to release him.

"Did I get an apology? No!" raged the
Professor. "Señor Sombrero said I
reminded him of a boy at school who'd
kicked his cat and threw me out of the
country."

"I wish someone would throw you out
of ours!" retorted Emily H.

"Odious child!" spluttered the
Professor. "You stopped me from finding
the tarantula THIS TIME! But you
haven't found it either and one day, some
day, I shall find it!"

Maybe it was the shouting that woke

him, but just then Theo peered out of the knapsack.

"That's my tarantula!" screamed the Professor.

At the word "tarantula" havoc broke loose amongst the passengers.

"AAAH!"

"HELP!"

"SAVE ME!"

The passengers dived under their seats or tried to climb into the luggage racks. The Captain came running from the cockpit, and grabbed a newspaper.

"Don't panic! I'll squash it!"

The Professor saw his chance. He reached for his killing bottle. "Leave this to me!"

Emily H raced down the aisle. "Don't

come a step closer! Don't you dare!'' Theo
clung to her. He was all of a tremble. She
turned to the passengers.

"Not everyone likes spiders, I know.

But by my life, Theo is totally lovable. He has the funniest sideways walk, he spins silk of the finest gossamer, and when he curls up in a ball, he's adorably sweet.

Look, I'll show you."

Emily H held out her hand. At once, Theo climbed down from her shoulder and curled up on to it.

"Ooh!" the passengers sighed.

"Do you *really* want the Professor to kill him and cut up his corpse? Yes or no?" asked Emily H.

"No! No! No!"

Now all the passengers were weeping, except for Professor Pinkerton. He saw his last chance fading, and lunged forward with his killing bottle. Emily H kicked his shins, hard, and he fell flat on his face.

"Grrrrr!" he roared. "Odious child!"

"That's enough from you," said the Captain. "My passengers have given their verdict. Theo shall live."

He confiscated the killing bottle and made the Professor sit by himself at the back of the plane. Then he sent a radio message to say he had a child on board with the biggest spider in the world.

When they landed, the news was out and the Media were waiting. Flashbulbs popped and TV cameras zoomed in.

"They only want to see you, Theo. There's nothing to be scared of," said Emily H.

But Theo seemed to enjoy the fuss. He puffed himself up so that he looked his biggest.

The Professor gnashed his teeth in a jealous rage. He strode out before the cameras. He was tall, and had the air of a very important person.

"I am Professor Percy Pinkerton," he said. "I have studied spiders all my life. That tarantula is a rare specimen. I want to study it for the Sake of Science. This child as good as stole it and I demand it back. By rights it belongs to me!"

"Theo doesn't belong to you! He belongs to himself!" said Emily H.

The Professor put on his oh-so-clever smile. "You're just a child. What do you know?"

Emily H saw that Theo was shaking. For the second time that day his life hung in the balance.

It was true that she was only a child and Pinkerton was a scientist who knew many things that she didn't.

"But I know all I need to know!" she said.

Her eyes were on fire. Her voice was like thunder.

"What I know is this:

"My name is Emily H and cold steamed spinach is my favourite food and I live in a castle with Pottle and my favourite creatures are spiders and you have killed hundreds of them and you must promise RIGHT THIS MINUTE never to do it again."

In the same breath she told the Professor to take off his shoes and socks and hold up his hands so she could see he didn't have his toes or his fingers crossed.

Professor Pinkerton turned to the crowd. He was waiting for them to laugh at the odious child, but they didn't.

"Go on, Professor, promise!" everyone shouted.

The cameras zoomed in. He was on TV. If he refused to promise, the Professor knew that in the eyes of the world he would indeed seem a cruel-hearted murderer. He took off his shoes and socks and put on a smile as if to prove he was a truly lovely person.

"I promise," he said, and slunk off through the crowd.

When he got home, Edwards was waiting with a grin. He'd seen the Professor on TV. "I've got you on video, Prof. Do you want to see yourself?" he asked.

"No I don't!" snapped the Professor. He stormed out and slammed the door on Edwards' chuckles.

At that moment in the castle next door, Emily H was climbing into bed. She

gave a big yawn. "I'm totally happy,
Pottle," she said. "Mission accomplished.
True or false?"

Pottle gave a fluttery sigh, and smiled.
"You're an extraordinary child, Emily H."

But Emily H was already asleep with the
biggest spider in the world on the pillow
beside her.